My Name is NEVAEH

DARLENE K GATTO

Artwork by Sherrie McKenzie

Archway Publishing books may be ordered through booksellers or by contacting:

Archway Publishing
1663 Liberty Drive
Bloomington, IN 47403
www.archwaypublishing.com
844-669-3957

ISBN: 978-1-6657-2874-4 (sc)
ISBN: 978-1-6657-2875-1 (e)

Library of Congress Control Number: 2022915179

Print information available on the last page.

Archway Publishing rev. date: 11/15/2022

As I unlocked the door of the townhome and walked down the hallway, I could hear my baby girl, Nevaeh, crying outside in the backyard. As I headed to the back door, I passed the sofa and found my wife, Jade, passed out in another drug-induced state of mind, oblivious to the world around her. I went outside and found my baby girl in the far corner of the yard with a little bit of shade covering her small body. She was sobbing softly as I picked her up, her diaper dripping wet and her skin red from the sun. I was livid; how long had she been out there? I was done with my wife; this was the last time she would neglect our daughter. I picked up Nevaeh, carried her inside, washed her little face, fed her, and gave her some milk. I took my daughter upstairs and bathed my little treasure. I put recovery gel on her skin to keep the sunburn to a minimum and took her next door to my neighbor, who was a sweet, godly woman. She had just written her first book, titled *My Best Friend*, and had given it to Nevaeh. I went back into the house, packed a few essentials for Jade, and carried her to the car. I drove her to the recovery center and checked her in for six months. I called my boss and asked for an emergency vacation, as I would be deployed in a few weeks. I took Nevaeh and went to a small town in Texas where my mom and dad lived. I explained the circumstances of the last few months and asked them to keep Nevaeh for me in a guardianship position until I got back from deployment. They loved Nevaeh, and it was no hardship on their part, so of course they would take her. The few remaining days before I had to leave were wonderful. Nevaeh was so happy, not asking for her mother at all and not caring she had not seen her for days and weeks. She was excited to be there.

Early the next morning, I left for Iraq, and that was the last time I saw my baby girl. While I was driving in Iraq with a buddy of mine, my life ended when I drove over a land mine. Nevaeh would never know how much her daddy loved her, except through his parents. I had left a nice life insurance policy in Nevaeh's name only, and my parents put it into a trust account for her until she was eighteen and out of school. She grew up on my parents' farm where she loved playing with the animals and had the love of my mother and father. She grew up hearing about me every day; they told her of my walk with God and that someday I would see her again. Nevaeh loved her little corner of the world with her father's parents but was always curious about her mother. As she grew older, she would talk to her grandmother about her, but her grandmother did not know much more then Nevaeh did—just that her name was Jade. Her grandparents were getting quite old by the time Nevaeh's graduation came and went. They loved her so much and always told her about her best friend, Jesus. Nevaeh grew to love him so much that by the time her grandparents died, Jesus was her only friend. In tears and feeling so alone, she sold the farm and went to Washington State to find Jade, the mother she never knew.

Jade woke up in the drug recovery center and tried to remember how she had gotten there. Her head was going to explode. She was scared and wondered where Nevaeh was. She thought, *Oh God, where is my baby?* She broke down in hysterical tears. How had this happened to her? How had her world become so complicated?

For the next ten to fifteen years, Jade found herself in and out of the recovery center, wishing to God she could get rid of this beast inside her. In her more lucid moments, she would think of her baby and husband, and that would send her on another spiraling roller coaster into hell. She would get some relief from the monsters inside of her through the drugs that would make her forget and live in a world where there were no problems and no consequences for her part in Nevaeh's life. One day Jade had had enough; she was done, and she was going to end it all forever. *At least*, she thought, *I will be free*. Jade slit her wrists in one final attempt to get rid of the voices inside her. Her next-door neighbor, Jan, heard her scream as she fell to the floor and called 911. Jade lived through that encounter with death. Jan took her home and nursed her back to health. She told her about a man who had died on the cross for her sins and how much he loved her. Slowly over time, Jade got better and better with the help of her neighbor. Jade came to know Jesus as her best friend and Savior.

It was a cold and rainy day in Seattle when Nevaeh got off the plane. Over the years, she had kept in contact with the wonderful woman who had taken care of her all those years ago. She called her from the airport that morning and told her she was in town to find her mother and see if she could help her. The lady, Jan, told her to come to her house straight away; she had a long and wonderful story to tell her.

Jan called Jade and told her Nevaeh was in Seattle and that she was looking for her mother. Jade started crying in remorse for all the years she had lost with her daughter; she also knew this young lady may never want to claim her as her mother, but Jade felt she had a new friend in her world, and she could trust them with all her heart. She also knew Jesus would help her through this hard time, and she would not have to rely on drugs or herself to get through this. Jade hung up the phone and fell to her knees, sobbing and begging Jesus to forgive her for abandoning her little girl all those years ago and, if there was a way to make up for the lost time, to please give her the wisdom and courage to do this for Nevaeh's sake. After a while, Jade, totally and emotionally drained, got up from the floor, cooled her face with a cold cloth, and walked next door where she waited for her daughter's return to her world.

In the meantime, Nevaeh was praying a similar prayer as she rode in a taxi to Port Orchard. She had a deep faith and knew God was in control of this day, but she was still excited and nervous at the same time. Would her mother claim her as her daughter, or would the woman who'd given birth to her reject her yet again? Nevaeh took a deep breath to steady her pulse and asked God to give her the courage and wisdom to get through the next few hours. Three hours later, the taxi stopped in front of Jan's house, the neighbor lady who had taken care of her all those years ago. Nevaeh slowly got out of the car and looked up at the house as the taxi pulled away and drove down the road. "It's now or never," she said to herself.

Nevaeh knocked on the door of the Jan's house, not knowing her mother was inside and not imagining they had remained neighbors for all these years. For you see, when Nevaeh's father was killed, part of his life insurance had paid off the house that Jade was living in. Jan opened the door. Nevaeh said, "I'm the little girl you took care of all those years ago. My name is Nevaeh."

"I know your name, dear. Please come in," said Jan. "It is so lovely to see you again after all this time." She put her arm around her as they started walking down the hallway. As they came into the living room, the lady said, "Please, dear, sit down. You must be very tired after your trip. How about I make us some tea."

Jade walked out of the bathroom. She heard voices in the hallway and thought, *Nevaeh must be here already. Oh, dear God, help me not to blow this encounter with my daughter.* Nevaeh looked up as the door opened and Jade came out of the bathroom.

"This is my neighbor," Jan said. "Dear," she said to Jade, "would you like to have some tea with us?"

"Of course," Jade said.

Nevaeh told her host, "I probably should call a hotel and make reservations for tonight. May I use your phone?"

"Nonsense," said Jan. "You can stay with me. It will be like old times when you were a little girl."

Nevaeh said, "I don't want to impose on you, but that would be wonderful. Are you sure?"

"Of course, dear," Jan said. "Follow me." Nevaeh took her suitcase from the hallway and followed the dear lady up the stairs, vaguely remembering her surroundings from somewhere long ago in her memory of another world, another lifetime. She put her suitcase on the bed, turned around to the dear lady standing behind her, and gave her a hug that felt like it had been a lifetime coming. Nevaeh knew this lady still loved her, and her world felt safe once again.

Jan and Nevaeh fell into some sort of routine just getting to know each other all over again. Nevaeh knew God would open the way for her to find her mother again. She was content for now just to be with this dear lady again. Days turned into weeks and months; the neighbor lady dropped by so often that Nevaeh began to feel they were all one happy family, but in the back of her mind, she knew she needed to start looking for her mother. One evening, they were all sitting outside on the back porch and Nevaeh asked the dear lady if she remembered her mother. Perhaps she could tell her about her mother.

Jade knew what was coming; she knew it was time to tell her daughter the truth. Jan went inside, and Jade took Nevaeh's hand and told her she needed to tell her something. With tears streaming down her face, Jade told Nevaeh who she was and about the journey she went through to get where she was now and how Jan had kept her informed of her little girl in Texas. Jade begged Nevaeh to please forgive her for not coming after her and giving her a mommy when she was a little girl. Jade told her about the drugs and the demons that caused her such pain and sorrow. Jade told her how, in the end, she found Jesus and learned to love and forgive herself.

By the time Jade finished her story, tears were rolling down Nevaeh's face. They were tears of joy; now she had found her mother and knew in her heart she would never be alone again, ever. Jan came back outside and thanked God for his greatness in bringing these two precious people back together. There was so much laughter and crying that evening. Nevaeh was exhausted and could feel in her heart that God was going to do great and wonderful things for the three of them. She kissed them both good night and went upstairs to her room.

Early the next morning, Nevaeh made herself some coffee and took it outside on the back patio. She barely slept at all the night before. She was so excited she had found her mother. She knew deep in her heart that God had orchestrated this whole wonderful thing, and she was trying to figure out how all three of them could live together forever and eternity. Nevaeh went back inside, and after she was finished with her coffee, she went upstairs and took a shower and lightly made up her face. She was so lovely inside and out she didn't need much makeup. A plan was beginning to form in her mind, she just needed to talk to her mother and Jan.. She thought, *what if my mother and Jan sold their houses and then the three of us together bought a house?* Each of them would pay equal amounts on the mortgage. Nevaeh could not wait to talk this over with these two women whom she loved dearly. She bowed her head and asked God to lead her and give her wisdom. Jan and Jade thought Nevaeh's idea was brilliant, and they set in motion to sell their houses that very day. A lot of work had to be done to get both houses ready for the market. They each made a list of what had to be done: wash the carpets and windows, touch up the paint, and stage both homes.

Nevaeh spent the better part of two weeks helping her mother and Jan get their houses ready to sell, and at last, they were done. So when the houses went on the listing website and the date for the open house was scheduled, all three ladies decided to celebrate. They booked a hotel on the shore and just relaxed, especially dear Jan, who had worked extremely hard the last two weeks.

The morning sun peeked its way across the water and lit up the room Nevaeh was sleeping in. It was so quiet at the shore that all three ladies slept far into the morning and would have slept longer had the screeching seagulls not awakened them. Nevaeh stretched, threw her comforter off, and went to the kitchenette where she made some coffee and looked out over the water, she watched the birds dive into the ocean. It was breathtaking, like a sweet glimpse of heaven. She would have stood there for a long time, but she heard footsteps and then the shower turned on in the adjoining room. She needed to hurry if she was going to beat her mom and Jan to breakfast. Nevaeh felt so blessed, so loved, she wanted to share it with the whole world. She felt in her heart and spirit that God was leading her in a direction that would involve children. Children that did not have a chance at a happy life, or the adults in their world were hooked on drugs and were sick in their minds. Nevaeh felt God had saved her and her mother for this purpose in life. As Nevaeh and her mother, Jan too of course, where driving home, she shared with them what she felt God was calling her to do. Jade was concerned it would bring back old memories in her own life she had put to rest. Nevaeh said, "Yes, Mom, you may be right, but God and I will be with you, and Jan too. We have been blessed in finding each other, and I feel the three of us can help little children in foster care. I have researched it, and we can have four to six children at one time, and maybe more with Jan's help."

So the three ladies prayed God would lead them to the children that needed them the most. Within the next two weeks, Jan and Jade's homes were sold at asking price, and they began the search for a new home for themselves and the children that would come into their world. They would need six or more bedrooms with the same number of bathrooms. They prayed God would lead them to the perfect house. They would need a big backyard with lots of room to play. So the journey began. Jan, Jade, and Nevaeh looked for a home for three to four weeks and finally found one in Gig Harbor, Washington, that met all their needs. It was a good thing because their old homes were getting close to closing for the new owners, but because the ladies paid cash for their new home, they were able to get in sooner than normal. It was a lovely older craftsman home with a massive front porch and master suite on the ground floor, with a huge great room flowing into the dining room and kitchen. It had a half bath on the ground floor as well, and all the other bathrooms and bedrooms were on the upper level. It was so beautiful and cozy. The ladies thanked God and started to unpack the boxes and place the furniture. It was hard and backbreaking work for the three ladies as they set up each room for the children to live and play in. They were only going to take three children to start, so, of course each little one had to have their own bedroom. Before the end of the month, the ladies finally had "Dave's Home" ready for the children. All three ladies felt Nevaeh's dad should be involved in some way. And that was how it became a home for little children who had already lived a lifetime in their short years. Nevaeh contacted the state to see what requirements they would have to fulfill to become a licensed foster home. The ladies were so excited and prayed daily for God's leadership and direction. As they went through the training and orientation to license their home with the state, they felt the need to rest and wait for God to open the door. They had no idea how long that would be, especially since they had decided to only take foster siblings and not individual children. Spring had turned into summer when Nevaeh got the call that there were three little siblings, two little girls and a baby boy, needing care, ranging from six months to four years old. Nevaeh said a quick prayer. Were these the little ones God had for them? She felt in her heart they were, and said, "Yes, we will take all three of them." So little Amy, who was two years old, and Darla, who was four, and tiny little six-month-old John came to live with Nevaeh and her mother. Jan was getting older, so she was taking it easier, but still could give so much love to these precious children. It was a beautiful sunny day when the man brought the children to Dave's Home, and Nevaeh felt her dad was looking down on her as the car pulled into the driveway. The children were so quiet and looked so sad, it brought tears to Nevaeh's and Jade's eyes as they waited for the man to get the little ones out of the car. Jade took the little bundle, baby John, out of the man's arms and thanked God for another chance to love a little baby again. Nevaeh took little Amy's and Darla's hands and started walking into the house as the man brought in three little paper bags—all the children had in the world. Jan was a hot mess when she saw that and had to leave the room until she could compose herself. There were no tears when the man left, and Amy would not let go of Nevaeh's hand, but Darla did. She had to make sure this was a safe place for her little brother and sister. Tears rolled down Nevaeh's face as she observed Darla taking care of her siblings in such a way. She knew this was not the first time this little girl had taken on this responsibility. It broke her heart, and she vowed she would take that burden from little Darla's shoulders. Nevaeh, determined in her heart, knew she would give these babies all the luxuries she could afford and more love than they could contain.

Darla looked Nevaeh in the eye and said, "My little brother cries a lot, and my little sister is scared of the dark."

Nevaeh said, "That's ok. It will always be ok."

The ladies got the children settled in their own rooms but felt, for the first night, it would be ok if they all slept in the same room. Nevaeh and Jan stayed with the children while Jade started dinner. Watching Darla and Amy explore the upstairs was heart-wrenching as they went from room to room, asking questions and wanting to know how long they were staying. It was in that moment, Nevaeh knew in her heart she was going to adopt these little children. Darla started to relax a little as they all went downstairs for dinner. There was so much to see that the girls ate very little for dinner, however, John made up for it. After dinner, Jade and Jan took the children upstairs and bathed them while Nevaeh cleaned up the kitchen. The children were asleep when Nevaeh went upstairs. She told Jade and Jan she wanted to talk to them in the playroom. When the ladies were sitting comfortably, Nevaeh shared with them the idea of adopting the children and asked them how they felt about it; this was a lifelong decision, were they up for the task? Unbeknownst to each other, they were all feeling that God called them to do this. So it was decided, and the very next morning, Nevaeh called her attorney to start the process to adopt these three darlings. Her attorney called her later that morning and told her it might be more difficult than they had imagined; both parents were still alive, and the legal battle might get a little rough. Nevaeh did not care; God would make a way. Darla, Amy, and John became life's purpose for these three wonderful ladies. They looked for ways to bring laughter into their little hearts. Darla started to become a little girl again, not a parent as she was when she came to Dave's Home. Fall was just around the corner, and Halloween was a few short days away when Jan began to get sick. Jade took her to the doctor and the results had come back. Jan was terminally ill with stage-four ovarian cancer and was given a short time to live. Nevaeh did everything in her power to make sure the Christmas present she had planned for Jan would come to pass. Baby John was crawling by the time Thanksgiving came and went. Jan was bedridden by this time, and little Darla would crawl up beside her and read books to her for hours and hours. Nevaeh and her attorney were working hard to get the adoption done before Jan went home to be with Jesus. The children's father was in jail for killing someone, and the mother was a drug addict who had left the state, but getting them to sign over their parental rights was proving to be quite difficult. The father eventually terminated his rights. They were still waiting for the mother's signature. Christmas was a week away when Nevaeh's attorney called her. He told her the children's mother had been found but she had died of an overdose. Nevaeh was sad to hear this; she may have died without knowing Jesus as her Savior. Her attorney told her to come and sign the adoption papers stating Darla, Amy, and Baby John were hers. There were tears of joy and sadness on Christmas morning when Nevaeh gave Jan her Christmas present; a framed copy of the adoption papers.

It was a bitter cold evening in late January when Jan passed away. Darla had a hard time with her passing, feeling lost and sad that her "Nana Jan" was not around to play with or talk to her anymore. Amy and Baby John were far too young to understand what was happening. Jade and Neveah were glad Jan wasn't in pain anymore, knowing one day they would see her again. January turned into February, and snow was on the forecast, which was a good thing because it would take little Darla's mind off Jan's passing. All three children were excited about the coming snow, but they would need new snow boots, mittens, hats, and warm coats. Darla wanted a purple coat, Amy wanted a pink one, and Baby John didn't really care. On February 13, eight to ten inches of snow dumped on

Gig Harbor. The children were ecstatic as they put on their new coats, mittens, and boots. All bundled up, they went outside to build a snowman. It was priceless to hear their laughter and voices of excitement. It was a beautiful winter wonderland with the sun just peeking out of the gray skies. Baby John followed his sisters all around the yard. He would walk a few steps, fall into the snow, and then laugh and get back up. They all knew dear Jan watched from above.

Time passed quickly, and soon spring was here. Spring break was coming up, so Neveah and Jade thought it would be a good time to go on vacation for a week or so. The question now was where to go? Do they go to the ocean or the desert? The children had seen the ocean many times but had never been to the desert. So the desert was going to be their destination. Jade booked flights to Phoenix, Arizona, for the second week of April. The children were so excited; this was going to be there first vacation ever. Darla could barely contain herself, and Amy was just as excited. Baby John knew something good was happening, so he laughed and giggled as he followed his sisters all around the house. Darla and Amy knew they were flying to Phoenix, which, to them, was just as exciting as the vacation. They both kept asking how big the plane was and what held it in the air. Jade and Nevaeh explained to them as best they could, but the girls quietly chatted between themselves as they listened to the two women who loved them and Baby John more than anything in the world. The ladies knew it was going to be difficult to get the children to sleep. It was way past their bedtime when, finally, everyone was in bed and asleep. The next morning, the children arose early, just as excited as they were when they went to bed. They rushed through breakfast, squealing with laughter and energy. Getting them dressed and ready to go was a frazzled chore. Finally, everyone was in the car and ready to go to the airport. By the time Nevaeh and Jade got to the airport and got the children settled on the plane, they wondered if they had bitten off more than they could chew, figuratively speaking of course. They landed in Phoenix and rented a car to make the drive to Scottsdale. It was so beautiful and warm, and sunshine poured in through the windows. For once, Darla and little Amy were quiet and looked in wonder at everything that passed by. Baby John fell asleep in his car seat. The quiet setting was blissful.

As Nevaeh drove, she thanked God for her mom and the children, and prayed their little vacation would be wonderful, and they would have a safe return to Washington. It was late when they finally arrived in Scottsdale, and they soon found a nice Holiday Inn. The children were tired; it had been a long day. So Nevaeh and Jade fed them, bathed them, and put them to bed. They were asleep before their little heads hit the pillows. Sunshine woke Neveah, similar to when she, Jade, and Jan had been to the ocean before. Although this time, instead of screeching seagulls, she heard the peaceful cooing of little doves on a power line. Nevaeh quietly got up, made coffee, poured herself a cup, and took it out on the deck where the sun shined bright and warm on her face. She sat there and talked with her best friend, Jesus, and thanked Him for all the wonderful people in her world. Little Amy had awakened and opened the sliding door to come out and snuggle in Nevaeh's arms. It was all Nevaeh could do to keep from crying in sheer love for this little girl God had given her. Amy was chatting about whatever little girls talk about when you can't understand them, and soon Darla stuck her head out the door and said Baby John was awake. Peace and solitude were gone. Nevaeh kissed Amy, put her down on the deck, and went in to get Baby John before he woke up Jade. All the children talked at once about what they wanted for breakfast and what they were going to do first, second, and third on their vacation list.

Jade woke up and walked in to such an endearing scene that it brought tears to her eyes. She was so happy and grateful for what God had done in her little world. The children were eager to get done with breakfast so they could go out and jump in the pool at the hotel. Of course, sunscreen and bathing suits were the first things to be put on their little bodies. Darla looked like such a doll in her pink suit, Amy wore a yellow suit and looked like a sweet daffodil, and Baby John was in a swim nappy. Jade and Nevaeh followed the girls to the pool; Nevaeh carried Baby John, and Jade carried the bag that held the regular assortment of children's toys, floats, sunscreen, snacks, and liquids. The children laughed and splashed in the kiddie part of the pool until close to lunch time, when, finally, Nevaeh said, "Let's go eat lunch and have a quiet rest time."

Soon one day led to another. The children began to have a sun-kissed glow on their little bodies. It was so restful and peaceful that Nevaeh began to think she was in love with this desert and wasn't sure she could bear to leave it. Jade was beginning to fall under the spell of the desert as well. She loved the sunsets. The sunrises were something to behold as well, majestic in their own way. She had never encountered such dry warmth on her skin, she was in love with this desert. Soon it was time to pack up and go home to the rainy weather in Gig Harbor. Jade had looked at the forecast while she was helping pack up the children's belongings, and the thought was slightly depressing. She was going to talk to Nevaeh the first chance she had. An idea formed in her mind: why not spend the winter months in Scottsdale, and then after the children were out of school, spend the summer months in Washington? She thought it was a fabulous idea and couldn't wait to approach Nevaeh about it.

Just as forecasted, it was very cold and rainy when the plane landed at SeaTac. The children were grumpy, and Jade and Nevaeh's dispositions weren't much better. John was cranky, and the girls were bickering about whatever little girls bicker about. It was not a very happy scene. Nevaeh said a prayer and asked God for peace and patience to help her transition the children back to the rainy environment. However, it was slow going as the freeways were packed and gridlocked everywhere. Soon, thank God, the children fell asleep. Jade took this quiet opportunity to talk to Nevaeh about her idea. Nevaeh thought it was a wonderful idea as well, however the children would have to finish the school year in Washington, and it would take at least that long to sell their house and buy one in Scottsdale. Nevaeh loved her mother so much and was grateful she was thinking on the same lines. They wouldn't tell the children till they got home and rested.

Later in the week, Nevaeh and Jade told the girls to come into the playroom while Baby John slept so they could get their opinion on something. Darla and Amy came into the playroom right away. The ladies shared their idea with the two girls and asked what they thought.

Darla was in shocked that the adults in her world would even ask if something worked for her, then she understood what they were saying and was ecstatic. Little Amy was bounced up and down because her big sister was so excited about something Amy didn't yet understand. So it was settled; they would sell the house in Gig Harbor and move to Scottsdale in a couple of months. Amy finally got the gist of what was going on and said she wanted a pool and a puppy. Darla chimed in and said she wanted horses and other animals. The ladies thought they would move closer to McDowell Mountain where it would be slightly cooler. Both little girls were disappointed when they found out they would have to finish out the school year in Gig Harbor. Nevaeh and Jade found a lovely five-bedroom and three-bath home close to Scottsdale. They listed their Gig Harbor home with an agent and within a week it was sold, leaving the ladies with a ton of organizing and packing to do before school ended. So, by the time school had ended with the exception of a few snow days, they were ready to go. They trailered Nevaeh's SUV and gave the movers their new address in Scottsdale. Soon it was time to take a taxi to the airport. The children were beyond excited, singing songs Nevaeh and Jade had taught them the whole way to the airport. Darla's favorite was "Jesus loves me," and she sang it a little off key but with all her little heart and at the top of her lungs. It was a good thing the taxi driver had children of his own, so he wasn't too annoyed by the time they arrived at the airport. However, keeping all that energy in the children controlled was proving to be a difficult task. They were wonderful children but beyond excited; they knew they were moving to Scottsdale. Nevaeh and Jade wished Jan were with them because she always had a way of keeping the little ones quiet and entertained. Soon it was time to board the plane, and thank God, the children were quickly put on board. Nevaeh held Baby John on her lap, Darla was seated next to her, and Jade and Amy were seated across the aisle. As the plane took off, the girls squealed with delight and Baby John hung on to Nevaeh for dear life. As the plane leveled out for the short two-and-half-hour flight, the girls occupied themselves with crayons and colorings books. Nevaeh and Jade had always kept electronics at a minimum. Finally, with twenty minutes to go before touching down, Baby John fell asleep in Nevaeh's arms. She took the baby sling out of her backpack and wrapped Baby John in it so when they landed it would be easier to finish wrapping it around herself. Hopefully this way, he would stay asleep.

Twenty minutes later the plane touched down in Phoenix. Since they were in first class, they got off first. Nevaeh stood up, finished wrapping Baby John in the baby sling, took Darla's hand, and led the way up the ramp and into the terminal. The girls held each other's hands and chatted all the way through the terminal. Nevaeh rented a SUV like theirs with a car seat and a booster seat. The little family drove a half an hour to their new home in Scottsdale. Darla and Amy couldn't wait to see the house that would be their home for the rest of their lives. It was a beautiful view as they drove up the little mountain to their home in a cool lowland where mesquite trees grew wild and giant saguaros towered over the SUV. Nevaeh and Jade purchased this house sight unseen but felt the Lord had guided them in their decision. As Nevaeh stopped the car in their driveway, she felt a peace she knew had come from God above. Darla and Amy jumped out of the car squealing and running, trying to see everything at once. Nevaeh called the girls back to help unload the car. Soon everything was in the house and the girls were free to explore. Baby John stayed close to Nevaeh and Jade as this was all new to him. Later the girls came into the kitchen as Jade was fixing hotdogs, their favorite. Baby John sat on the floor next to Nevaeh and munched on his own hotdog she had cut into small pieces.

After lunch, all five of them explored the house and around the pool outside. By this time, the sun was starting to go down, and there was a slight chill in the air. So they all went inside the house and into the great room, which had a massive fireplace covered in river rock. Earlier, on the way to the house, they had stopped at Costco and purchased supplies they would need before the moving truck could get there. So, while Jade made a fire in the fireplace, Nevaeh found the sleeping bags they had purchased. Darla's was pink, Amy's was yellow, and Baby John's was sky blue. The ladies had nice puffy downy ones. Nevaeh put padding under them since the wooden floors were too hard to sleep on. Baths were done, and it was time to crawl in the sleeping bags. Nevaeh and Jade talked quietly into the night about how Jan would have loved their new home and about what the Lord had in store for their little family. Thank God it was the beginning of summer; they didn't have to worry about school for quite some time.

The morning sunshine streamed in through the windows, warming up the great room. Nevaeh felt little hands on her face; Amy was awake and hungry. So Nevaeh and Amy tiptoed to the kitchen to start the coffee and get pancake batter ready for the other children and Jade when they woke up. Jade awoke to the smell of coffee, and hearing a little chatter in the kitchen, headed in that direction. Nevaeh sat on the floor drinking coffee. Amy sat beside her, coloring in her coloring book. Jade stopped in the doorway of the kitchen and watched the scene for a while, she thanked God with all her heart for bringing her daughter and these three little treasures into her world. Darla and Baby John came up beside her. Amy squealed with delight when she looked in the kitchen and saw her sister and baby brother. Nevaeh got up and changed the baby while Jade fixed pancakes for breakfast. Nevaeh picked up the sleeping bags and moved them to the corner of the great room. Soon it was time to explore the surrounding areas around the house and pool. The girls were ecstatic as they ran around the yard, chatting between themselves about the animals they were going to get. The moving truck came two weeks early, which was so wonderful because it felt like an early Christmas to have their home full of furniture again. Every day, the girls swam like little mermaids in the pool, and of course, Nevaeh and Jade had enrolled them in swimming classes on their second day in Scottsdale. Summer turned into fall, and soon it was time to enroll Darla in school. Amy wanted to go too, so Nevaeh put her in a three-year-olds' class for three days a week. The children loved the climate and the mountains surrounding their home. The privacy was amazing. They adopted two big pit bulls to keep the yard and surrounding area safe. Nevaeh found a lovely church to attend, and the children were delighted with it as well. October was coming up, so it was time to think about what costumes the children wanted to wear for the harvest festival at their church. Amy wanted to be a daffodil, Darla wanted to be a good fairy, and Baby John was going to be an inchworm. Nevaeh and Jade had quite a bit of work to do, and even with all the help of the volunteers, it was going to be a tight schedule to get everything done before the festival.

Soon it was time for the children to get ready for the harvest festival. Nevaeh and Jade helped each of the little ones put their costume on and then into Nevaeh's SUV. As usual, the girls chatted between themselves and Baby John just held his lamby and looked out the window. It was a wonderful fall evening. The girls were so happy; this was the first harvest festival they had ever attended. Nevaeh was so thankful she could give these little treasures many first experiences with her and her mom. However, she was concerned that they needed a male figure in their world, but all the men in her life had passed away. A tear slid down Nevaeh's face. She casually wiped it away, and hoped her mother had not seen it. That evening, Nevaeh knew she was going to take this concern to her Lord and Savior.

Meanwhile, hundreds of miles away in Seattle, John, the children's biological father, had just received a pardon from the governor. The police sergeant had taken a liking to John and believed he was innocent. New evidence had come to light that revealed the children's mother had become a drug addict after she had given birth to Baby John. Her friend, not a good friend of course, had killed their drug dealer and framed John. John came to know Jesus as his personal Savior while he was in prison, and the first thing he was going to do when he got out was find his children. When he was arrested and sent to prison, Baby John was just four months old. John knew he had a long road ahead of him, but he knew his Savior would lead and guide him, and because he was falsely accused, he was awarded a sizeable settlement. John hired an attorney and told him his story. It took six long months to locate his children. He missed and loved them so much and was concerned about their well-being. So he decided that the best thing for him to do was to move to Scottsdale. He could slowly integrate himself back into his children's world. So John applied for a job and was hired at Darla's school.

Meanwhile, Nevaeh was having troubles of her own. There was a tiresome man from her church who had his eye on her. He had asked her many times to have dinner with him. Each time, she politely refused, wanting only to take care of her children and mother. This had been going on for about six months now, so by this time the man was literally stalking her. John now attended Nevaeh's church too, and everything soon came to a head. One day, after the morning service and Jade had just left to get the children from children's church, the tiresome man approached Nevaeh and stated he was not going to take no for an answer anymore. He grabbed her wrist tightly to make his point. John had been watching the whole scene unfold from a distance away, but when the man grabbed Nevaeh's wrist he knew he had to intervene. John casually walked over to Nevaeh and told her the pastor would like to speak with her, then asked her to come with him. Still visibly shaken, she replied, "Of course."

He gently took Nevaeh's elbow and escorted her away. As they walked by the man, John, who was big, tall, and muscular, whispered, "Don't ever touch her again."

He spoke quietly told Neveah he had watched the scene unfold, and he was deeply sorry for what the man had done. Nevaeh explained he had been bothering her for some time now, and she was quite frightened by him. John took Nevaeh to their pastor and explained the situation. The pastor was concerned that a man in his congregation had put his hands on a young woman in the church parking lot. He told Nevaeh the man was one of the worship team members and that he would take care of the situation. John and Nevaeh thanked the pastor and walked away.

Nevaeh thanked John and asked him if he would like to have coffee with her; she had a proposition for him. He replied he would like that as he too had a lot to talk to her about. Nevaeh thought that was rather odd because, although she had seen him many times at Darla's school and at church, this was the first time she had spoken to him. So they agreed to meet the next day at ten a.m. at the Starbucks in Scottsdale closest to her home. John arrived early and prayed that God would open the door for him to share his story with Nevaeh. He was dying to hold his children in his arms again. He thanked God many times over for this wonderful woman that had adopted his little ones.

Nevaeh walked into the coffee shop and spotted John in a corner next to a window. He stood up as she came toward him and helped her into her chair. They made small talk for a while before then John said, "I have something to show you." He told her God had divinely orchestrated the pardon granted by the governor of Washington. God had led him in this direction.

Nevaeh took the paper, and after reading it halfway through, looked up at him with fear in her eyes. She said, "What do you want? You can't take my babies from me; I adopted them."

As she rose to leave, John touched her hand, and said, "Please sit down. I would never in a million years take the children from you. You are the best mother and friend they could ever have."

Nevaeh, shaken to say the least, replied, "I don't understand, why did you find us then? How did you find us? What do you want now?"

John just smiled. He replied, "Nothing, I don't want anything from you but to get to know my children. I want to be around them as much as I can, as much as you will let me."

Nevaeh bowed her head and said a prayer in her heart. She felt God leading her. She looked up at him with peace-filled eyes and said, "John, I invited you for coffee to ask you if you would come and live in our guesthouse so there would be a man on the property and around the children. I never dreamed you were their father." Both were visibly shaken. They got up from the table and walked outside, relieved their talk had gone so well.

John went back to his rental, gave notice, and cleaned it out. When he returned the key, he told the landlord she had been wonderful. Then he drove straight to Nevaeh's home and thanked God the whole way for his mercy, grace, and all the miracles that have taken place to get him here. He drove into the driveway, and the two dogs were not happy he was there. Baby John was waddling around the fenced-in yard, while Amy had just returned from preschool. Nevaeh called her mom on the way home from picking Amy up to prepare her for what had happened and what was going to happen with John. Having been only three-and-a-half years old when Darla last saw him, Jade wondered if she would recognize him. Nevaeh and John had both decided not to tell the children about their parentage until they got to know him better. John parked his car and walked over to where the ladies were standing. Jade looked at him and felt such peace it brought tears to her eyes. She thanked God her little treasures would have their dad around them again. John was nervous and excited to see his babies. He wanted to run over and pick them up and never let them go. Although he tried to restrain himself, he still teared up a little when he saw his son and daughter. Nevaeh introduced him as John, the man that would live in the guesthouse. Amy shook his hand and John's knees about buckled. Her hand was so tiny, and she was so beautiful with long flowing blonde hair and green eyes. Baby John stood just behind Nevaeh and looked at him. So John got down on his knees, started playing peekaboo with him. He was soon rewarded with a little giggle. He knew he had found a friend in his precious little son. John anticipated seeing Darla but remembered school wasn't out yet. Instead, he went to the little guesthouse that would be his home for who knows how long.

Darla got off the bus to see a strange car parked in the driveway. She went in and told Nevaeh she had a good day, and asked if she could please have a snack. She was eating her snack at the breakfast table when John walked into the kitchen. Darla looked up and eyed the stranger; there was no recognition on her young face. Nevaeh again introduced him as John, the man that would live in the guesthouse. Soon Baby John waddled up to his dad and John turned around and picked up his son. Darla wasn't sure how she felt about that, but decided it was ok because her little brother seemed to like this man. Darla finished eating her snack and ran to change into her play clothes. She was excited to get outside and see the animals.

Soon a pattern formed for the little family. John already felt like a part of the family; the children adored him, and Nevaeh and Jade thought he was pretty special as well. Summer was almost here, Darla would soon be six. She had talked of having a little pony for so long, Nevaeh thought she would get her a small one for her birthday. She asked John what he thought of it, and he thought the idea was spectacular. They both made plans to have one shipped to their little farm, which already had cows, horses, chickens, and goats. When the outside gate was closed, the chickens and goats had open access to the fields.

One day Darla came home from school very upset, she ran into her bedroom and slammed the door. Nevaeh quietly opened the door and asked what was wrong, if there was anything that had happened at school Darla wanted to talk about. Darla just shook her head before she broke down and started crying. Between sniffles, she said all the children at school had made fun of her because she was the only one in her class that didn't have a daddy to take her to school. She hated school and never wanted to go back. Secretly, little Darla had been thinking of a distant memory of her father, how she had felt loved and safe whenever he was around. So, when the children started teasing her at school, she couldn't keep the tears back any longer. Nevaeh looked up as John walked by the door and nodded her head. Now was the time. John entered Darla's bedroom, and Nevaeh left, quietly closing the door. John picked up his crying daughter and held her until she stopped crying and then wiped her eyes. He said, "Darla can I tell you a story, a true story about your birth mom and dad?" John explained to her what had happened to her dad. He was so sorry her birth mom was dead, but Darla had gotten over her mother's death a long time ago. She didn't know her dad was out of prison though.

"Where is he?" she asked. She wanted her daddy right now and started crying all over again.

This time John couldn't hold back his tears any longer, and He said, "Sweet baby girl, I love you so much. I am your daddy."

Darla just looked at him and then she saw it—a faraway memory of her dad calling her his sweet baby girl. Then the only tears that rolled down their cheeks were tears of joy. John just held her and thanked God over and over that she remembered he was her dad. He would tell Amy and Baby John soon as well. Glory to God! Darla's birthday that year was the best one she ever had for she had the most wonderful present ever—the love of her dad back in her life. She thanked her best friend, Jesus, daily for that. She had missed her dad so much, and unbeknownst to Nevaeh, little Darla had cried herself to sleep many nights thinking of her father.

The next day, a Saturday, was a beautiful sunny morning. Nevaeh awoke early that morning, made a cup of coffee, and made her way to the patio to talk to her Lord and Savior. She expressed her gratitude to have a home like hers with all the people she loved in it, which now included John. That shook her up a bit, because they were close friends, and she thought that was how it would always be. But that morning, her heart took a turn toward love, a new feeling she was going to talk to her mother about.

While she was deep in thought, John had awakened early and taken his coffee out on the patio as well. He watched Nevaeh as she was sitting outside. As he watched the sun come up and kiss her face, he thought she was the most beautiful and precious woman God had ever put on this earth. He'd known for some time now that he loved her and was going to stay close to her for as long as she would let him.

Nevaeh was sipping her coffee when the person she was daydreaming of walked over and sat down beside her, as they do many mornings. However this morning was different, John sensed it but couldn't quite put his finger on it. The atmosphere was different, but in a good way. As they talked quietly for a while, Nevaeh felt something different going on inside her. She was weary of these new feelings. They alarmed her; she'd never felt like this before. Nevaeh excused herself and went to her room while John stayed where he was. She needed to pray for answers and direction, so she stayed in her room until she heard the pitter-patter of little feet. She always left her bedroom door open in case the little ones needed her. Amy poked her head in and said "Momma Naia, I am hungry."

Nevaeh just smiled and thought, *What's new, Amy's always hungry.* She picked her little girl up and carried her to the kitchen where John had already started breakfast. Amy saw her dad and squealed with delight. Nevaeh gave John his daughter and finished cooking breakfast herself. John sat at the breakfast nook with Amy when Darla ran in and crawled on his lap too. It was a picture-perfect sight. It took Nevaeh back in time to her dad, who reminded her so much of John. In that moment, Nevaeh knew she loved this man more than anything in the world. Jade walked into the kitchen to see John and Nevaeh looking at each other like no one else was in the room, even though John was still holding both his daughters.

Jade just smiled and said a little prayer. God would work everything out in His timely manner. Then she went and poured herself a cup of coffee. The love spell was broken, and John and Nevaeh came back to earth.

"Mom," Nevaeh said, "I didn't see you come in. Did you sleep well?"

"Yes, dear, I did," Jade said, although she doubted if either of them would have seen a gorilla come into the room. Nevaeh and John just looked at each other and smiled.

Nevaeh heard Baby John moving around in his crib, so she went down the hallway into his room. She said, "Good morning, my sweet baby boy. I love you." She picked him up, gave him kisses, and changed his dripping diaper. Nevaeh carried the baby to the dining room and put him in his highchair. The girls came running in and took their seats at the table as well. Nevaeh and Jade brought in breakfast, while John brought in the coffee and orange juice. They all took their seats, and John led the prayer for breakfast and the day. Saturday was special this way; everyone could have breakfast together.

Nevaeh and Jade were getting the children ready for church the next morning when John came into the playroom and told the ladies he would see them at church. The pastor needed to speak with him about something before service.

"Ok," Nevaeh said. "That will be fine."

No sooner had John left when the dogs began barking aggressively. Nevaeh told her mom to finish up with the children, and she would see what they were barking at. Nevaeh walked to the window in the great room and saw a car parked at the gate. Something was familiar about it, but she couldn't place where she had seen it before. A man got out of the car and stood by the gate as if he were trying to get in. The dogs went nuts and charged the gate. Tuffy, the bigger pit bull, tried to jump the gate to get to him. The man hurried back to his car, got in, and drove away. Nevaeh was beyond frightened. She would tell John about this the first chance she had. By then, Jade and the children came out, ready to go to church. They had no idea at what had just transpired, and Neveah didn't tell them. Everyone piled into the SUV, and they were on their way to church.

It was such a lovely service, and the worship was so amazing, that Nevaeh forgot to say anything to her mother and John about the incident. However, that night when everyone was asleep, it all came back to her and she prayed. She felt in her spirit that evil was lurking around outside. She stayed very still. She knew if anyone were out there, the dogs would bark. But she hadn't heard them for some time now, and she thought, *Maybe the dogs are not barking because they're dead.* Nevaeh couldn't sleep anyway, so she quietly got up and checked all the doors and windows in the house. As she was walking back to the bedroom, the man from earlier stepped out of the shadows. He looked at her and said,

"Nevaeh, why didn't you go out to dinner with me? Why don't you care for me? All of this could have been avoided, but now you know I am going to have to kill you for not caring for me, for not talking to me."

Meanwhile, John was restless and hadn't slept at all. It was past midnight when he sensed something was terribly wrong. He hadn't heard the dogs for a long time. John put his clothes on, got his glock out of the drawer in his nightstand, and quietly went outside. He almost tripped over the dogs. He bent over to shake them awake but knew they were dead before he even touched them. "Dear God, help us," he prayed. As he ran back toward the house, he glanced at the gate and spotted a car—it belonged to the tiresome man from church who constantly bothered Nevaeh. Their pastor had called John early that morning and said they needed to talk; the man had just been released from the mental hospital that morning. John looked through the window and saw Nevaeh was as white as a ghost and shaking like a leaf, but she was trying to stand strong. He had to get in there and knew where the key was to the back door. He got it, unlocked the door, and quietly closed it behind him. He went in the direction of the great room. The man was inching closer to Nevaeh. She was frozen with fear and couldn't move. "Dear God," John prayed. "Help me not to hit her."

He shot the man in the back of the leg; he went down and so did Nevaeh, who fainted. John quickly tied up the man and called the police and their pastor. Then he went to Nevaeh and held her gently in his arms. She was so white that John wondered if the man had hurt her. He prayed, "God, let her be alive. I love her so much."

Nevaeh awoke to John's arms around her and his declaration of love. *Maybe I'm hurt or dreaming*, she thought, but then she heard sirens. Everyone in the house heard them too. Chaos erupted. The children cried, Jade was hysterical, the police rang the doorbell, and the pastor called John to tell him he was on his way. John picked Nevaeh up, carried her to the sofa, and put a blanket around her. She was still in shock, still shaking like a leaf. Jade let in the police and EMTs. She was going to get Baby John when the doorbell rang again—it was the pastor. When Jade opened the door, she tried to control her hysteria, but when he shook her hand, she lost it again. The pastor wished he had brought his wife, but he didn't want to place her in danger. He took Jade over to a chair, and set her down. Then he went to find John.

John saw his pastor come into the great room and went to talk to him and the police. It was at that moment the children took the opportunity to pounce on Nevaeh, kissing and hugging her. "Momma Naia, we love you. We didn't want the bad man to hurt you," Darla said. Nevaeh just kissed and held them. She thanked God with all her heart that her treasures were not harmed. Soon the police left with the insane man. The pastor was on his way out when Darla ran up to him. She said, "Did you know Jesus didn't let that bad man hurt my mommy?" The pastor just patted her little arm and told her she was all right, God had kept her safe.

It took a while for Nevaeh and John to calm the children down. Jade was no help at all. As they tried to get them settled for bed, the girls insisted they were going to sleep with Nevaeh that night. Nevaeh assured them it was ok, but just for tonight. Both girls nodded and went to Neveah's bed. John slept in Darla's bed for the night. He was amazed at all the stuffed animals his little girl had in her room thanks to sweet Nevaeh. Because he was concerned about how it might impact the girls, he set the alarm on his watch so he could bury the dogs early in the morning.

John tossed and turned most of the night in the little bed, waking hours earlier then his alarm. He got up and buried the dogs, sad his favorite dog, Tuffy, had died. He went to the guest house, showered, and then walked back to the main house where he found Nevaeh drinking coffee in the breakfast nook. He sat down beside her. She leaned against him and thanked him again for saving her life.

"I didn't really, beautiful," he said. "God just orchestrated it all by having me here at the right time." Nevaeh just nodded then remembered the dogs. He knew what she was thinking. He told her the dogs had most likely been poisoned and he had already buried them. A tear slid down Nevaeh's face at the loss of their family pets. She knew Darla would take it the hardest. *Maybe we should get a puppy this time so it can grow up with the children*, she thought.

"I have an idea," John said. "Let's get a puppy for each of them, even Baby John, and let the children name them." Nevaeh looked up at him and thanked God that He had brought John into their world.

"I love it," she said. "Could we possibly do it today and have them delivered?"

John replied, "Or better yet, have the children pick them out from a breeder."

Soon Amy walked into the kitchen and saw John and Nevaeh sitting in the breakfast nook. John picked her up and asked her if she slept well. She nodded and snuggled closer to her father. Nevaeh got up and started Saturday breakfast to get the children's mind off what had happened the night before. Soon everyone was at the table enjoying the breakfast Nevaeh had prepared. John did his best to keep everyone's spirits up, but it was going downhill fast with everyone lost in their own thoughts. John looked at Nevaeh and she nodded. He smiled and explained that their family pets were no longer here, they had gone to dog heaven and they all must be very brave.

Darla nodded and said, "Ok, Daddy, we will." A tear slid down her little face anyway. Amy didn't say anything, and Baby John was playing with his food.

"John," Nevaeh said, "Don't you have a friend who might have three little puppies the children could pick out? They should be at an age to go to permanent homes about now." John let it sink into their little minds. Darla, the first one to understand, let out a squeal, jumped down, and ran around the table into her father's arms.

"You mean it, Daddy? You mean it? Little, tiny ones?" She looked at Nevaeh, and her mother nodded.

"You can pick out your own puppy and name it," she said. Darla was ecstatic. She jumped around to her little sister and tried to make Amy understand what their father and mother had said. Amy was jumping up and down too. She didn't know why, but it was fun, and everyone was happy. That's all she cared about anyway. So, after the dishes were done and everyone was dressed for the day, they all piled into the SUV, except for Jade. She hadn't slept well the previous night and needed some "me" time. Nevaeh gave her mom a hug and told her they would be back shortly.

They drove down the driveway and on to John's friend's house. Darla was singing "Jesus loves me" at the top of her lungs. She always did that when she was happy. Soon John pulled into his friend's driveway and everyone got out. Nevaeh took the baby and John held the girls' little hands. Nevaeh was glad John's friend was a collie breeder. The children fell in love with them and wanted to take all the puppies home with them, but their dad reminded them—just one per child. It was priceless to see Baby John waddling around the kennel area with one little black-and-white puppy playfully trying to climb up his feet. The puppy would fall, get back up, and try again; you could tell he'd already claimed his master. Both girls were on their knees giggling and laughing at the two little golden white puppies that were jumping on them. Nevaeh thought of Jan, who must be looking down from heaven on this precious scene. It was at times like these that she really missed her. John's friend said he would bring the puppies over later that day, and John said that would be fine. Then they all piled back into the SUV.

The drive home was anything but quiet with the girls telling their mom and dad what they were going to name their puppies, and even Baby John's puppy. Nevaeh didn't mind; she loved and needed it so badly.

The little family drove home and waited for John's friend to deliver the puppies. In the meantime, they had a lot of work to do. There was a little room off the kitchen that would work as a puppy room. So they put puppy pads on the floor in the far corner, laid blankets for each of them, and last but not least, put bowels of water in the room. When John's friend arrived with the puppies, the children went crazy. John had to quiet them down so they wouldn't scare the puppies. "*Shhh*," he said. "We have to use quiet inside voices, not outside voices."

The children nodded and sat quietly, each by their own puppy. It was such a sweet picture. Jade, as excited as the children, quietly got on her knees beside them. John and Nevaeh took the opportunity to walk outside and get some fresh air. They both knew they had to talk about the night before and about what was said between them. So John and Nevaeh talked about what had transpired last night, about their love for each other, and how they both knew God had orchestrated the whole wonderful and precious encounter.

Summer soon turned into fall. John and Nevaeh were sitting out on the back porch, there was a full moon that night, and the children were inside with Jade. They were just making small talk, content with being near each other, when John suddenly got down on one knee, opened a little box, and asked Nevaeh to marry him. It came as a shock! She hadn't expected this so soon, although it seemed like she had known him forever. She nodded her head and said, "Yes, I will marry you, my love." John stood up, drew his future wife into his arms, and kissed her for the first time, gently and sweetly. It was Nevaeh's first kiss from a man other than her father or grandfather. They walked back into the house and told their little family they were going to be married. The children didn't understand, but Jade did. She seemed to get more emotional as she got older.

She took both of them in her arms and said, "Thank God, it's about time." Not only was Thanksgiving two weeks away, but now Nevaeh and John's wedding was only days away.

It was beautiful and sunny on the day of the wedding. The leaves on the trees were painted in mixed shades of gold, red, and blue against a canvas of green. It was an outside venue. The guests were seated in white wooden chairs lined up on a grassy knoll outside of the farm. A long light white cloth was laid down the center aisle. The two little flower girls walked down the center aisle and threw red rose petals from their baskets. Then came Baby John and Jade, and last but not least, beautiful, sweet Nevaeh came down the aisle alone since her father was in heaven looking down on her. The wedding went as planned, and the children were on their best behavior. It was simply a fairy-tale wedding that God ordained from heaven above. Jade stayed with the children while John and Nevaeh flew to the islands, Maui to be exact, where they spent a short but wonderful week for their honeymoon. On the way back, Nevaeh told John they needed to bring the children here as well as her mom.

When they landed at the airport in Arizona, her mom and the children were waiting for them. "Dad!" Darla said as she jumped into his arms. "I never want you and Momma Naia to go anywhere without us again." Both parents agreed it would never happen again.

Soon it was just a few weeks before Christmas, and wanting this to be the best Christmas ever, John and Nevaeh agreed to get the biggest tree they could find for the great room. Christmas morning was beautiful and cold but still sunny. Nevaeh, John, and Jade had stayed up the night before long into the morning hours to get everything for a picture-perfect Christmas wonderland for the children. The tree, standing against the middle of the wall, was massive. It extended the length of floor-to-ceiling windows, which were draped with beautiful green garland. Three stockings hung on the fireplace: one of purple-pink velvet for Darla, one of yellow velvet for Amy, and one of blue velvet for Baby John. There were candles encased in glassware among the garland and holly berries on the mantel. The presents surrounding the tree that Christmas morning brought tears to John's eyes. He was so happy and grateful at what God had done in his world in such a short time. When the little ones came into the great room, you could have heard a pin drop. All three stood together holding hands with their mouths open wide. Darla stood in the middle and her little brother and sister were at her sides. A crackling sound from the fireplace snapped the children out of their trance. Darla pulled her little brother and sister along with her as she walked up to the Christmas tree. They shook their little heads. They couldn't believe what had transpired while they slept. John and Nevaeh laughed and cried at the same time as they watched the children. It was the children's first Christmas together with their dad, Nevaeh, and Jade. Jade came into the great room and watched the children as well.

Soon the presents had been unwrapped and breakfast done. Nevaeh cleaned the great room as Jade started on Christmas dinner. The pastor of their church were coming over for Christmas dinner with his family. His children were the same age as John and Nevaeh's. Christmas dinner consisted of a succulent roast with mashed potatoes and gravy on the side, and macaroni and cheese for the children. The pastor's wife brought a delicious salad and a butterscotch cheese-cake for dessert. There were homemade cookies and candies galore. A cheese tray was on the side table in the dining room as well as homemade bread. It was a feast to behold. When the family and their friends sat down for Christmas dinner that afternoon, they were grateful to God for His blessings and love. Everyone enjoyed the dinner, and of course, all the adults ate too much, especially the men. The children bundled up in light jackets, and Jade took them outside to play in the yard and look at the animals on the farm. Nevaeh, John, the pastor, and his wife went into the sunroom for after-dinner coffee. They chatted but it was mostly just small talk. Then the pastor told John and Nevaeh that the man who had tried to kill Nevaeh had committed suicide a couple of days before, and to the pastor's knowledge, the man had no parents or siblings. No one came forward to claim him and there was no one in the world who had loved him.

Nevaeh said, "That's where you are wrong, Pastor. He had Jesus, but his mind couldn't comprehend Him. He most likely needed a human form to convey that." No one said anything for a moment, and then Nevaeh continued, "I think we need to bury him. Just the four of us, not the children."

Astounded at what he had just heard, John looked at his new wife and said, "Are you serious? Did I hear you right?"

Nevaeh just smiled and nodded. "Yes, you did. How do you feel about it? It was his act of violence that brought our love out into the open. I think we should."

Pastor and his wife glanced at each other and nodded. "Yes," he said. "It would be a wonderful act of kindness." It was settled then, and within a few days they had a quiet memorial for the man.

December came and went, and life fell into a pattern for the little family at the base of McDowell Mountain. The children excelled in every aspect of their little lives, especially church and school. They were the love of Nevaeh and John's lives, and of course, Jade's too. School was ending for the year, and summer was on the horizon. John asked his beautiful wife what her plans were for the summer.

Nevaeh asked, with a twinkle in her eyes, "What about going to the islands for a couple of weeks?" She had told the family earlier in the month there was going to be another addition to their little family—she was pregnant. John and

Jade were ecstatic, but for different reasons. Little Amy and Baby John, who was now a toddler, didn't understand the concept of a new baby, but Darla did. She didn't want to share her mommy with anyone except her current little brother and sister. Darla had a habit of keeping little things inside of her heart until they became big things and exploded. However, the trip to Maui kept her mind off it for the time being. The children did exceptionally well on the long six-hour flight, and the little family arrived in Maui late in the evening. They found a lovely little house that they rented for a couple of weeks that was right on the ocean. However, there were cliffs and a forest within walking distance, so keeping a close eye on the children was a challenge, to say the least. Nevaeh was doing very well, but the morning sickness was giving her problems and limited what she could do with her family. Nevaeh couldn't bring herself to attend a specific outing John wanted to do as a family and thought it would be wiser to stay close to home. John was hesitant to leave her, but she convinced him she would be fine. "Take Mom and the children and have fun. I love you," she said and gave each of them hugs and kisses.

Darla had been very distanced with her affection since Nevaeh had told them all she was expecting. John and Nevaeh thought it was just a phase their oldest daughter was going through. John didn't want to go too far from Neveah, so he and Jade took the children on an adventure close by. Nevaeh took a few naps throughout the morning and was soon feeling much better.

She was out walking along the beach when John came running up to her and said, "Have you seen Darla? She was with us and now she's not."

"No," said Nevaeh in alarm. "But I slept quite a bit while you were out. Let me get my tennis shoes on and I'll help you look for her." After she got her shoes on, John took her hand and they prayed they would find their little girl safe and very soon. John and Nevaeh met Jade and the two little ones on their way to look for Darla. "Mom," Nevaeh said. "Take the children home and we'll look for Darla. We have our phones."

"Yes, dear. Please hurry; it's getting close to sunset," Jade said. Nevaeh and John hurried back to the place where John had last seen their little girl. Thank God John had the foresight to bring a huge flashlight, as there was no moon out tonight and a storm was rolling in. It was dark by the time they got to the spot where Darla had last been seen.

Meanwhile, Jade was anxious to locate Darla because the terrain was rough going where they had been earlier that day with the children. So she prayed and felt God leading her to call the police. She did and they arrived a short time later. The police were concerned about the absence of the little girl and called in as many policemen as they could spare.

The storm arrived in all its fury, and it frightened Nevaeh and John more and more by the moment. Nevaeh slipped and fell as she walked through the deep rain forest and called her daughter's name. John and Nevaeh had gotten turned around in the foreign terrain when the policeman found them. "Thank God", John said. "My wife is spent, and she is four months pregnant. Can you have one of your men take her back to our house, and I will continue to search for our daughter?"

By the time Nevaeh and the policeman got back to the house, he was half-carrying and half-dragging her. John called ahead to prepare Jade, so she watched for them and waited with the door open. The policeman lifted Nevaeh in his arms and carried her inside. Jade took Nevaeh's wet clothes off, put pj's on her, and then covered her with warm blankets in her bed. The policeman went back to help with the search. Jade had put Amy and Baby John to sleep long before the policeman had carried Nevaeh inside. Nevaeh was cold and shaking. Her stomach was killing her and she had abdominal cramps. She felt blood between her legs. As tears rolled down her face, she said, "I think I lost the baby." For once, Jade was not hysterical; she just sat and held her daughter and prayed that God would make something good come from all this grief. She got Nevaeh cleaned up and changed the sheets. She rested as best as she could under the circumstances.

Meanwhile, Darla walked behind her dad and little sister, Jade and Baby John were walking in the front of the group, when a beautiful blue and purple butterfly flew in front of her. She adored butterflies, and this one was the biggest and most beautiful one her little eyes had ever seen. She followed it down a little hill and then up another little hill before it flew away. Darla turned around to catch up with her family, but nothing looked the same. So she just kept walking. *Maybe I will find them soon*, she thought. By the time Darla found the little path she thought they had all crossed earlier in the day, it was dark, and she was in a strange place. She knew she was lost, but she continued to walk around in a circle toward the cliff that was close to their rental. It poured down rain and she couldn't see. She tripped and fell twice. She cut her little knees, and they started bleeding.

Finally, she couldn't go any further because she literally had hit the side of the cliff. Darla couldn't see anything, but she heard waves crashing around her and felt water on her face. She was a smart little girl, far beyond her years in wisdom, and she knew she had to climb higher because the tide was coming in. Her dad had told her this their first day on the island. She climbed higher and higher until she couldn't hear the waves crashing anymore. It was late and had stopped raining when she found a resting place on the side of the cliff—a shelf about four feet wide and three feet long. Darla was soaked to her skin but thanked her best friend, Jesus, for this spot where she could rest.

The morning sun kissed Darla on her little face. She woke up and realized she wasn't in such a safe place. This little girl, who loved God with all her little heart, prayed He would please forgive her for her attitude toward her mom and the new baby. That He would please help her father find her and get her off this cliff.

John was spent; he had been looking for his little girl all night and had slept on the couch when he came in that morning so as not to wake Nevaeh. He woke up to seagulls screeching and thought he heard his daughter yelling for help. He put his tennis shoes on, ran outside, and found Darla on the side of the cliff, not more than ten feet from the house. He ran back inside, grabbed his phone, and called the fire department. He then ran back outside toward his daughter, climbed the cliff as high as he could go, about ten feet below his daughter, and told her how much he loved her and how brave she was.

Darla was hungry and damp from the rain, but she was happy her dad had found her. And what does this little girl do every time she's happy? She sang her favorite song "Jesus loves me" at the top of her lungs.

Nevaeh awoke to the sound of her little girl singing. She woke her mother, told her to watch the children, and then ran outside toward the voice of her daughter. She stopped in her tracks because there were two fire trucks on the beach with their ladders extended to her daughter and her husband. Darla was still singing when she was carried over to Nevaeh's arms. Then and only then did this brave little girl start to cry. "Mommy, Jesus was with me all night. He gave his angels charge over me," little Darla said. The firemen got John down, and he came running over to his wife and daughter. He held them in his arms and thanked God for the safe return of his daughter. John didn't yet know Nevaeh had lost the baby. *Now was not time to tell him,* Nevaeh thought as she held her daughter in her arms. John carried them both into the house and sat them on the sofa. Then he went back outside and thanked the firemen for rescuing his daughter.

It had been a trying night for Jade with the death of her unborn grandchild and another grandchild missing, so when she saw Nevaeh holding Darla she couldn't keep her emotions controlled any longer. She sat down and burst into hysterics. Nevaeh and little Darla just looked at Jade. They knew that after a while she would be fine. John came into the room just as Jade was getting her emotions under control. He smiled at his precious wife and daughter and held them in his arms once again. By this time, Amy and Baby John had woken up, and when Amy saw her big sister she ran and gave her a big hug and asked all about her adventure.

God was good to the little family from McDowell Mountain. They flew back to their little farm. Nevaeh and John were sad at the loss of their unborn baby, but they both knew God works all things together for good. The girls went back to school and were extremely happy; they loved school so much. Nevaeh and

John told the children that, sometimes, God doesn't let babies get born. Instead, he takes them back, but when he does, he *always* gives something better. So, this time, there were going to be two precious little babies joining the little family—Sandy and Sammy. Indeed, God had blessed John and Nevaeh with their family. And this is the story of Nevaeh.